HAZEL TOWNSON

IGNORANCE

is

Andersen Press • London

For the dedicated staff of the Children's Hospitals Appeal Trust, in acknowledgment of the wonderful work they do.

First published in 2001 by
Andersen Press Limited
20 Vauxhall Bridge Road, London SW1V 2SA
www.andersenpress.co.uk

British Library Cataloguing in Publication Data available
ISBN 1 84270 042 1

Phototypeset by Intype London Ltd
Printed and bound in Great Britain by the
Guernsey Printing Company Limited, Guernsey,
Channel Islands

Your library is precious – Use it or lose it!

1

A Question of Taste

Amy Bliss's first kiss was a huge disappointment. It tasted of pickled onions and tobacco.

Luke North had been smoking since he was twelve years old and ate pickled onions with practically everything except Christmas pudding. Amy found his second kiss even worse as he breathed out rather heavily just before it. Also, they were standing under a tree; something had just dropped onto Amy's head from a branch above and was crawling across her scalp. Normally she would have screamed and clawed madly at her hair, but courage! This was supposed to be a sacred moment, to which she was still giving the benefit of the doubt.

The third kiss got frozen in mid-air because by then the crawling had reached the top of Amy's ear and she panicked. Pushing Luke aside, she performed a sort of hysterical war-dance with much shaking and striking of the head. This dislodged a massive spider onto her chest, whereupon she screamed blue murder and was sick all over the bluebells.

As for Luke, he coolly lit a cigarette and sauntered back to the disco in search of a less fidgety partner and a cheese-and-pickle sandwich.

Walking home later for a sleep-over with her friend Chloë, Amy revealed her disillusionment in vivid detail, finally declaring:

'If that's sex you can have my share. I don't know what all the fuss is about, and

I've gone and snagged my new top on that stupid tree.'

Chloë had listened to the tale with growing concern and was busy piecing together certain scraps of information she had gleaned from eavesdropping on the conversations of her older sister Lauren and her friends. At last she asked in a hesitant little whisper: 'Did you say you were sick straight after he kissed you?'

'As a dog! I can't stand spiders. The very thought of that thing crawling all over me . . . ugh!'

'Then – aren't you worried?'

'Not now, but I certainly was then. That wretched thing could have crawled right inside my clothes.'

Chloë sighed. 'I'm not talking about the spider. But don't you realise? If you were sick something serious could have happened.'

'Oh, it has. I've gone right off Luke North. I wouldn't go out with him again if he was the last boy on earth.'

'I don't mean that, silly! I mean something really mega. Something that could change your life for ever more.'

Amy looked genuinely puzzled. 'What are you on about?'

Chloë gave an exasperated sigh. 'Don't you know anything, Amy? You could – well, you could have caught AIDS!'

'AIDS!' Amy laughed incredulously, which only increased Chloë's concern.

'Surely you've heard of AIDS?' she insisted. 'Honestly, Amy, you can't be that innocent!'

Chloë reckoned she was infinitely more streetwise than Amy, having the advantage of frequent gleanings of Lauren's drama-laden gossip.

'I heard our Lauren telling somebody that AIDS is what you catch when you get sick after you've been canoodling. Well, that's you! Lauren reckons it's the worst disease you can ever get. They haven't worked out a cure for it yet.'

'Don't be daft!' retorted Amy, though

4

slightly less confidently than before. She pointed out that there had only been two kisses; nothing more. They hadn't even held hands. Surely that wasn't enough to bring you down with AIDS?

Or was it? The teacher had talked about AIDS when they were studying reproduction in a biology lesson last term but Amy had been too embarrassed to listen properly, let alone take it in.

'Things like that don't happen to people like us, and besides . . .' she began, eager to reassure herself. Yet the sentence petered out in dismay as Chloë solemnly nodded her head. Chloë was enjoying the drama, the feeling of superiority and worldly wisdom, not to mention gratitude that she wasn't in this mess herself.

'As soon as you get home tomorrow you'd better tell your folks,' she advised.

'WHAT?'

'Don't sound so horrified – they'll soon get used to the idea. They'll look after you. You'll probably get spoiled to death like invalids always do. Anyway, look on the bright side. You'll be able to leave school.'

'I don't want to leave school, I want to be an astronaut.' Amy stood for a moment in rising panic, contemplating a future which might just be turning grotesque.

'Chloë, you shouldn't go around saying things like this unless you're absolutely sure. It's very upsetting. How would *you* like it if somebody suddenly told you were going to die?'

'Oh, I'm sure all right,' insisted Chloë with confidence, 'and it's always best to face up to things. No use burying your head in the sand. People are bound to find out pretty soon and our Lauren says . . .'

But Amy didn't want any more third-hand advice.

'I think it's horrible, frightening people like that,' she cut in desperately. 'Anyway, how come you think you're so well-informed?'

'Pity you haven't an older sister,' retorted Chloë smugly. 'Every girl should have one. I don't suppose Eileen, being only your step-mum, is quite the same as a real mum at a time like this, and dads are useless.'

Dads!

Any groaned, suddenly picturing herself turned out of the house in the middle of a stormy night by her own disgusted dad, after the fashion of some Victorian melodrama.

'All the same, if I were you I'd tell Eileen first, since she's the nearest you've got to a mum. Me and our Lauren always go to Mum first when we're in trouble. With a bit of persuasion and plenty of tears you can win Eileen over, then she'll be able to get round your dad. She'll tell him for you and think up a good excuse. That's what mums are for.'

Real mums, maybe, thought Amy, seeing her whole life breaking up before her eyes like a spilt jigsaw puzzle. There was no way she would ever confide something like this in her step-mum. Anyway

Eileen and her dad always stuck together like superglue. Eileen would support her dad even if he said let's blow the house up and claim the insurance.

The prospect of facing this united front, even with the mere suspicion of such a tragedy, was so awful that Amy started chewing her imitation-ruby good-luck beads. A gypsy fortune-teller had sold her these at Barnsley Fair, charging her always to wear them if she wanted a tranquil life. Amy chewed so hard that she bit through the thread and watched the spilt beads go bouncing down the lane like brittle drops of blood.

Accepting this at last as a final proof of doom, she wailed: 'I only went out with Luke North to take my mind off the maths test. I don't even like him. In fact, right now the very thought of him makes me feel . . .'

She had been going to say 'sick' but decided she'd better not in the circumstances.

Chloë laid a comforting arm around her friend.

'Well, you've always got me.' She felt generous and strong, loyal and noble – a selfless heroine and a present help in trouble.

'I'm here for you now, and I'll still be here when the next bad thing happens. Our Lauren reckons misfortunes always come in threes.'

It was the final straw. Amy burst into noisy tears.

'Oh, come on now, cheer up! Nothing's ever as bad as it seems,' comforted Chloë. 'You should count your blessings, starting with this sleep-over at ours. At least that's going to give you time to calm down and sort yourself out before you have to face your folks. Besides, once we get home you'll be able to consult our Lauren. She's sure to have a few ideas. She's a star at breaking terrible news gently.'

Which, to Chloë's bewilderment, made Amy howl even louder.

2

The Bluebell Test

'Lauren! We need your help,' whispered Chloë, poking her head round her sister's bedroom door. 'We think Amy might have AIDS. Come and talk to her, will you?'

'She what? Oh, the poor kid!' Lauren shot across the landing like a Scud missile. With nothing to do but her nails she'd been feeling in desperate need of a bit of excitement such as this.

Amy was slumped on the spare bed in Chloë's room looking as if she had only days to live. Lauren settled down beside her and put on her Caring Form Captain's voice.

'Listen love, it's not the end of the world, you know. Even famous people get AIDS and there are lots of experiments going on to find a cure. Who knows, in another few years . . .'

Amy's only response was to howl like a dying dog.

'Is she sure? Has she taken the test?' Lauren asked Chloë.

'What test?'

'The bluebell test. You hold this flower under your chin and if it turns blue you've got AIDS.'

'If what turns blue?'

'The skin under your chin, silly!'

'That's buttercups, to see if you like butter.'

'Same principle. I heard a woman whispering it to her friend in the Post Office queue. We've some bluebells in the back garden. Go and get some.'

Chloë was back in no time with a fistful of limp flowers.

'Hold your chin up, Amy! Oh, come on, don't be such a baby!'

Lauren jiggled a bloom around Amy's Adam's apple.

'There! It's positive all right. Let's try another one just to be on the safe side.'

By now Amy was almost hysterical.

'Don't cry, pet! I'll come with you to tell your folks if you like. I'm ever so good at it. Last term I went home with Greta Shaw when she'd been suspended for a week and her mum was quite reasonable about it. She gave us milk-shakes and waffles. I guess she didn't like to make a fuss because I was there.'

From what was now the deluge of Amy's sobbing a few gasps turned into words. 'Can't – tell – Eileen – can't – tell – anyone.'

Lauren decided to be firmer. 'Oh, come on! There must be somebody you can tell. Who's the person you can talk to best? The person who'll really understand you and not just fly off the handle?'

'I guess it's her gran,' suggested Chloë. 'She gets on great with her. Don't you, Amy?'

Amy nodded miserably, but that was enough for Lauren.

'Right then, go and see your gran. I'll cover for you tomorrow. I'll ring your folks and tell them Dad's taking us all to the zoo as it's a special one-day holiday and you're invited.'

'Her gran lives in Peacebourne. She'd have to go on the train.'

'So?'

'She's got no money. We spent up at the disco.'

'No problem; I'll lend her some out of my Christmas savings. How much will she need?'

Ignoring Amy completely now, Lauren and Chloë between them began planning her immediate future. They worked out roughly what the fare to Peacebourne would be and added on a bit extra for emergencies.

'I'll go with her,' offered Chloë.

'No, you won't! I haven't that much money,' protested Lauren. 'It's my turn to buy the gerbils' food this week and I need some new eyelashes. Anyway, Amy could do with a bit of privacy when she's talking to her gran. This is a very delicate matter.'

So it came about that very early next morning, before the town was properly awake, a shrivelled-looking Amy boarded a north-bound Virgin train, waved a brave goodbye to her childhood and began a trek along the corridor in search of a secluded seat wherein to lick her wounds.

Throughout a sleepless night she had tried desperately to remember all she had ever learnt about sex and horrible diseases. She had even crept downstairs to consult Lauren's biology book which she had spotted on top of her homework pile on the kitchen table. However, she had had to flee before finding the right information as she thought she heard somebody coming.

This had merely doubled Amy's panic, but there was no way she was going to risk seeking advice at home. Surely that bluebell test was nothing but an old wives' tale? Yet at least it emphasised the fact that some educated, reliable first-hand information was certainly required; reassurance at best, or solace and practical support at worst. That meant a heart-to-heart talk with the only possible candidate – Gran.

The very thought of warm, loving, dependable, all-knowing Gran made Amy feel a whole lot better. Gran would sort out this bewildering, frightening mess in no time. The best thing to do right now was just to find a secluded seat and keep calm until the train arrived at Peacebourne.

In the third compartment Amy came across a boy sitting by himself, looking even gloomier than she felt.

Could it be . . .? Yes; it was!

Recognising her favourite cousin, Amy cried out before she could stop herself: 'Harry! What on earth are you doing here?'

Harry Bliss looked up in guilty alarm like some nobbled shoplifter, then suddenly relaxed again.

'Oh, it's you, Amy! You scared me to death! Anyway, I could ask you the same thing.'

Amy hesitated. In the circumstances it might have been wiser to avoid her cousin altogether, but the damage was done now. On the other hand, it was a great relief to have someone to share the journey with. She took a deep breath and said: 'As a matter of fact I'm going to Gran's.'

'Hey, so am I!'

This coincidence seemed to stun them both into silence. Then, as the refreshment trolley trundled into view, Harry said, 'Well, sit down, for goodness' sake! You're blocking the gangway.'

Amy sat.

She had to admit she was fond of Harry; he was the brother she'd never had. They had shared much of their childhood as their two families had always spent Christmas and summer holidays together, especially a couple of weeks in Torquay each August. Harry was really good fun and Amy had always felt she could trust him.

Well, up to a point, she amended now. There were some things you didn't tell, even to a near-brother. Still, Harry deserved some sort of explanation.

'I'm not just making a social visit,' she said at last. 'I want Gran's advice. I've hit a bit of a crisis and I reckoned Gran was the best person to turn to.'

Harry sighed deeply. 'You and me both,' he agreed.

3

Loss of Face

Harry's dad and Amy's dad were brothers. Amy had always been fond of Uncle Steven and his wife, Auntie Fran. They had always seemed to be lovely, loving people, generous, happy and totally supportive of their son. Amy would never have believed that Harry could acquire a problem big enough to need Gran's advice.

Yet Harry's problem seemed to him a life-shattering affair. It had begun one morning just after his dad had left for work. His mum had suddenly leapt up, whirled around the house, packed a suitcase, ordered a taxi and given Harry a suspiciously sentimental hug before being whisked away to the railway station. She'd made some excuse about visiting a sick friend and not being sure just when she'd be back but Harry could see at once that she was lying. She actually had tears in her eyes, suggesting that this might even be goodbye for ever.

Naturally, Harry had tried to question his mother but she'd claimed she was at the last minute and had no time to talk.

'All will be well, you'll see! Just don't worry about a thing!' she had cried with a brave attempt at jolly reassurance. 'I've stocked up the fridge, taken my library books back and reduced the milk order by a pint. Oh, and I've left the window-cleaner's money on that shelf above the microwave.'

With a far from reassuring wave she was then borne away to a private clinic to have a face-lift and certain other bits of cosmetic surgery. This was a closely-guarded secret which she planned to share only with her husband, and that not until later in the day when it would be too late for him to protest about the cost, the risk, the inconvenience and the fact that he liked her the way she was.

Meantime Harry had spent an anxious day wondering what was really going on and how his dad would react. This 'sick friend' had never been mentioned before and Dad had left as normal that morning, obviously expecting to come home to the usual welcome.

Dad took the news even worse than Harry expected, despite (or maybe because of) having found a somewhat enigmatic note on his pillow. He spent most of the evening pacing up and down the hall waiting for the telephone to ring, and when it did he sent Harry next door on some lame pretext so that his conversation couldn't be overhead.

Naturally, Harry had continually pestered his dad with questions but no satisfactory answers were forthcoming. There was just a tenseness like the prelude to some major volcanic eruption. Obviously some sort of a marriage breakdown was on the cards.

Had his mother left home for good? Was a divorce in the offing? Dad must have got rid of him so that he could have a terrible telephone row. The more Harry thought about it, the more depressing his suspicions grew.

He cunningly intercepted the post for the next few days, but there was nothing in his mother's handwriting; nothing helpful at all. No more incoming telephone calls either. What did eventually turn up in the post was an exorbitant florist's bill for Dad, who usually regarded flowers as a waste of money. But worse, far worse than that, was the fact that Dad began disappearing for whole evenings with the lamest of excuses, shunting Harry next door again to do homework (or otherwise) with his friend Paul.

Of course, Steve spent these evenings visiting the clinic armed with extravagant bouquets, but Harry didn't know that; Fran had forbidden Steve to tell their son what was going on until they knew how things would turn out.

'I want the New Me to be a complete surprise!' mumbled Fran from behind her bandages. 'I'm really looking forward to seeing Harry's face when he sees mine. Just tell him my friend's no better and I'm staying on to look after her. We can explain the true facts later.'

So naturally, after being kept so much in the dark, Harry's imagination ran riot. He pictured his dad having some romantic affair with a much younger woman. For let's face it, he had to admit his mum had been starting to look dismayingly wrinkled and middle-aged.

Harry had just made up his mind to follow his dad one night and find out who this woman – this evil marriage-wrecker – was, when the problem was settled for him. As he was peering out through one of Paul's next-door windows Harry spotted his dad's car arriving home with a woman in the front passenger seat.

This must be HER!

How dare Dad bring her to the house while Mum was away?

Harry's hate for this woman was already at fever pitch as he looked her over from his hiding place.

Unlike Harry's greying-haired mother, this creature had lustrous raven tresses and was much slimmer, shapelier and younger-looking, just as he'd suspected. It was growing dark and he couldn't see her face too clearly, but he did get a vaguely oriental impression as the security light came on.

(Flashback from a recent Triads film; could Dad be into drugs as well?)

Steve Bliss was very attentive, helping the woman from the car and guiding her up the steps into the house with a protective arm.

Monstrous!

As the hall light came on, Harry watched the pair of them fuse into a passionate clinch before the front door slammed shut on this outrageous treachery.

Disgusting! Utterly disgusting!

That was when Harry grabbed his pen and scribbled a seething note to say he was spending the night at Paul's and might be very late home from school next day as he had a Chess Club meeting. Pushing the note through his own letter-box Harry went straight to the station to look up times of trains to Peacebourne.

Just wait till Gran heard what was going on! She'd put a stop to this nonsense and talk some sense into Dad. And if that didn't work, maybe Harry would stay in Peacebourne and live with Gran for ever more. That would show them!

So now here he was, sitting in a

speeding train opposite his favourite cousin Amy, plucking up courage to confess. Amy was a kind-hearted sort, and having had to come to terms with a step-mum she was bound to understand his trauma. Harry had to admit he was pretty desperate for a shoulder to cry on.

With a catch in his voice he blurted out at last:

'My parents have split up. Talk about a shock! Mum's walked out and Dad's got another woman, somebody a lot younger than Mum. I suppose it had to happen one day. I think she's Chinese.'

4

A Train Too Far

'I don't believe it!' wailed Amy, believing it passionately all the same. For let's face it, her confidence had been shattered. She was an expert by now in the way that Life could beat you down and trample you underfoot just when you least expected it.

'Life's a pig! An absolute pig!' she declared with feeling, taking care, though, not to reveal her own possible predicament. 'It's a good thing we've got somebody like Gran to turn to.'

'You're telling me!' agreed Harry. 'She's

a rock! Always has been. You can tell Gran anything and she's never shocked.'

'Never flies off the deep end.'

'You mean handle.'

'Never criticises,' added Amy pointedly. 'Never judges.'

'Always listens properly and really cares.'

'I've never known her fail to come up with the right answer. She's so wise, she knows everything.'

'Absolutely!'

('We hope!') added Amy silently as she peered anxiously out of the train window.

Seeing the railway embankments covered in bluebells she closed her eyes and added tetchily: 'I wish we'd hurry up and get there!'

Yet when they did finally arrive at Peacebourne's tiny village station the train didn't stop. It simply hurtled through at a speed which set the lupin pods exploding all along the dithering wooden platform.

Amy was completely taken aback.

'Didn't you ask if it stopped at Peace-bourne?'

'Didn't you?'

'I've not been here on the train before. We've always come in the car.'

'Should have checked though, shouldn't we?' Harry was definitely dismayed, though trying to rise above it. He must set a good example of macho calm. 'Anyway, it's not the end of the world. We'll just have to get off at the next station and catch a bus back.'

'Oh, that's such a waste of time!' wailed Amy. 'I've got to be back home by tonight.'

By now she was anxiously chewing her nails.

'So have I, but it's no use getting into a panic.'

They sat in silence for the rest of the journey, each pondering their own lack of care and the possible consequences of this latest disaster, while secretly acknowl-edging that the real culprit was Fate, Life, Destiny . . . whatever you cared to call it.

And by whichever name, it certainly was a pig.

When they finally did leave the train it took them a while to find a bus station and to track down the number of the bus they needed. Then they discovered that the fare would swallow every penny of their joint resources.

Harry shrugged. 'If we need any more money we'll just have to borrow it from Gran.'

'I've already borrowed the train fare,' Amy complained.

'So have I, but it's all in a good cause.'

'Well, I suppose we've cracked it now; nothing else can go wrong.'

Which is an assumption nobody should ever make, especially after breaking their good-luck beads.

They finally arrived at Gran's isolated bungalow, having had to trudge the last half-mile up a muddy country lane – an unpleasant surprise as in the happy past they had always been dropped off neatly at the door by car. Then, adding insult to injury, they were confronted by a new dilemma.

Gran had moved away!

5

A Phantom Female

'Now then, where's Harry?' Fran had asked, emerging at last from her home-coming clinch the previous evening.

Steve had explained that their son would be next door at Paul's house, hope-fully getting on with his homework.

'He's had to spend quite a lot of time there lately, though I don't suppose he minds. Harry and Paul go back a long way.'

Giggling in delicious expectation, Fran demanded to have him back home at once.

'I'm dying to see his reaction.'

Wandering into the hall on the way to summon his son, Steve came across the note sticking out of the letter-box and smiled as he read it.

'That boy has a lot more tact than I gave him credit for. He's staying the night next door so we can have a bit of time to ourselves. I knew he'd guessed what was going on but I didn't credit him with this much sensitivity.'

Although disappointed, Fran was finally persuaded not to ruin this chivalrous gesture.

'All right then, you and I will keep this evening for ourselves and have a big celebration tomorrow instead. A special meal with Harry's favourite food and all the trimmings.'

So far so good, yet the following morning, when Fran actually read the note for herself she didn't like the idea of Harry coming home late from his Chess Club. She had waited long enough to surprise her son. He would have to cancel this meeting or it would curtail the celebrations and spoil everything.

With this in mind she sent Steve next door very early, to catch Harry before he left for school and ask him to change his plans.

But of course Harry wasn't there. He was already halfway to Peacebourne on the early train.

When questioned, Paul tried bravely to cover up for his friend.

'Er – he's already left for school.'

'What? At this time in the morning? That's not like our Harry! Why didn't he wait for you? You haven't quarrelled, have you? Been seeing a bit too much of one another?'

'Oh, no! Nothing like that. I just think he had – er – something special to do before lessons.'

'Such as?'

'Dunno!'

Steve frowned in confusion. This was so

unlike Harry who never left for school until the last possible minute.

'Right then,' he decided reluctantly, 'I suppose I'll have to see if I can catch him up.'

'Oh, I wouldn't do that if I were you . . .!'

'Why on earth not?'

'Well, you see, it's something very private. Kind of, a surprise.' Paul was floundering badly.

Baffled and highly suspicious, Steve was now determined to drive over to school to deliver his message in person and find out what was going on. But of course his son wasn't there. Hardly anyone was there. It was far too early.

Perhaps the lad had made a detour on the way and simply hadn't arrived yet? But no; Harry hated walking to school and would always take the shortest route.

Then Steve recalled Paul's mention of a surprise. Perhaps Harry had gone off to the twenty-four-hour supermarket to buy a present for Fran. He couldn't have missed the commotion of her arrival home last night. Ten to one he'd watched the whole thing through Paul's window. And after all, Harry was a thoughtful lad; could always be relied on for a tasteful Mother's Day present or a special birthday surprise.

Well, the next best thing was to button-hole a teacher and pass on a message asking Harry not to stay on for the Chess Club. Unfortunately, the teacher Steve buttonholed explained that the Chess Club had been abandoned more than a year ago for lack of interest.

Fresh alarm! What on earth was going on? And where was Harry? Not knowing whether to be furious or panic-stricken, Steve sped back home and caught Paul about to leave for school. And this time, loyal friend or not, Paul was forced to confess that Harry had gone to see his gran.

'All the way to Peacebourne?'

'Well you see, he's got a bit of a problem he wants her to sort out.'

'What sort of a problem?'

'W-Well, er, I'm not awfully s-sure,' stammered poor Paul, suffering tortures of embarrassment and doing his best not to look Steve in the eye. 'It's kind of private. Something about a love affair, I think.'

6

Ordeal by Fire

Gran's house had a weather-beaten 'For Sale' board in the garden, across the middle of which was pasted a much cleaner strip reading 'Sold'. Worse still, a glimpse through the living room window showed that most of the furniture had gone.

'I don't believe it!' roared Harry in disgust. 'She's lived in this house for forty years. Who could have guessed she was going to move? I never thought to ring up first to say I was coming. Don't suppose you checked either?'

'I had other things on my mind.'

'Same here.'

'Well, we could try ringing the doorbell,' Amy suggested. 'Gran might still be in there, finishing the packing. It looks as though there are still a few items left.'

They did ring, many times, but there was no response. They then prowled all round the house peering through every window, keyhole and letter-box but were forced to conclude that it was all a waste of time.

'It's no good; she's definitely gone.'

Amy flopped down on the doorstep. 'All that way for nothing! Now we're really in a mess!'

'Oh, come on, Amy! I've never known you to give up this easily before.'

'I know when to admit I'm beaten.'

'Beaten? We've hardly started!'

Harry was beginning to suspect that Amy's crisis must be even worse than his own. Quite a consoling thought, which cheered him up enough to hatch a brainwave.

'Come on, we'll try the estate agent's office. They'll be able to tell us where she's gone.'

'I doubt it. They won't give addresses out to any Tom, Dick or even Harry. We could be burglars or murderers for all they know.'

Nevertheless, Amy dragged herself to her feet, ready to clutch at any straw. Fishing a well-chewed biro from her shoulder-bag she wrote down the house-agent's address on the back of her hand.

'Dodge & Cheetham, 14 Clover Street,' she confirmed wearily. 'Come on then, I suppose it's worth a try.'

First they had to face another trek down the muddy lane and a long walk into the town, but at least Clover Street proved easy enough to find.

Yet here they faced another dilemma. Number 14 was boarded up, obviously having suffered a recent fire. Black smoke-stains edged what had once been doors and windows and in a side alley, flanked by police cones, lay a pile of charred debris.

'Can you believe it? They're burnt out! All their records must be gone!' mourned Amy, ready to burst into tears again. 'That's it, then; we'll just have to go home.'

'Not likely! I'm going to find Gran if it takes forever!'

'But our folks will be expecting us home tonight. We'll be in big trouble.'

'Well, there are different kinds of trouble. I don't know about you, but I can't feel any more desperate than I do already,' Harry declared with feeling.

'They'll tell the police. Before you know it there'll be search parties scouring the country for us. Helicopters even. They'll be out of their minds.'

'I doubt *my* lot will even have missed me. Anyway, even if they have, let 'em worry for a while. It's nothing to the worry they've put me through, I can tell you!'

'Another thing – what about our train tickets? Can we still use them if we stay until tomorrow?'

Harry scrutinised both tickets carefully.

'It's all right; they're period returns. That gives us three months which is fine by me. I'm not going back until I find her.'

'THREE MONTHS?' Amy couldn't help wondering if she would already be dead by then.

7

Sleight of Hand

Mrs Kate Bliss, grandmother to Harry and Amy, walked into the estate agent's office at 14 Glover Street to hand in the keys to her house and to enthuse about her new High Street flat. In a resonant voice she declared herself thrilled to be moving into a brand new property which was centrally placed and heated, bristling with all the latest gadgets and as far from muddy lanes as it was possible to be. In fact, she told the manager, it was the best move she could possibly have made.

As such enthusiasm was good for business, and as several over-hesitant customers were dithering about the shop, the manager encouraged Kate to stay chatting and even offered her a cup of coffee.

'The whole business has gone so smoothly,' Kate announced with fervour, thus earning herself a digestive biscuit to go with the coffee. 'Except for that fire in Clover Street, of course. I must admit that was a bit of a shock. When I read it in the paper I thought they meant this office. Easy enough to mistake a "C" for a "G" and the number was the same. Quite a coincidence really.'

'You can say that again!' agreed the manager. 'It gave me a bit of a turn, too, when I heard it on the radio. I jumped into the car and drove down here straight away, just in case.'

'I thought I'd have to start all this sales palaver at the beginning again, whereas now I've got a different problem which is why I've come to see you. It's all these modern gadgets,' Kate confessed somewhat shamefacedly. I can't get the hang of them at all. And I was wondering if you could suggest a source of help.'

She began bewailing her unfortunate encounters with several items of electrical equipment, which was far less to the agent's liking. He decided to cut short the chat after all. Luck was on his side, for just then Kate suddenly spotted a familiar face outside the shop. It was her son Steve, accompanied by a rather glamorous, slightly oriental-looking woman Kate had never seen before.

She ran out of the office, bursting with anxious curiosity.

'Steve? What are you doing here? My flat-warming party isn't until the end of the month. I do need a bit of time to settle in, you realise?'

All the same she gave her son an affectionate hug before demanding: 'Well, come on then, introduce me to your friend.'

'Mother, you know very well it's Fran!'

Fran, however, was delighted not to be

recognised. What a waste of money and effort if she had been!

'Hair colour makes such a difference, doesn't it?' she smiled kindly. 'But never mind me; we're looking for Harry. He's disappeared. Hasn't been to school today and wrote us an enigmatic little note with some lie about staying on for a meeting which didn't exist. He seems to be going through a strange phase lately. Growing up, you know.'

'Growing up a deal too fast if you ask me!' growled Steve. 'Got mixed up in some silly love affair. At his age, I ask you!'

'I guess it's partly our fault,' admitted Fran. 'We've had to neglect him a little bit lately. There were one or two things we weren't able to explain, which meant he was probably a bit confused. Circumstances kept us from paying as much attention to his problems as we ought to have done.'

'I didn't neglect him!' protested Steve.

'It's not neglect to let him spend time with his best friend.'

'Well, that's as maybe.' Fran waved a dismissive hand. 'But you must have had your suspicions about what those two were getting up to. Entertaining girl-friends behind your back.'

Turning to Kate, she added: 'Harry's friend Paul thought he might have come to Peacebourne to see you, so we drove up here straight away.'

'He was probably hoping you'd help him out of some silly entanglement.'

'Did you tell Harry I was moving house?'

'Well, no; you asked us to keep the whole thing secret so your flat warming could be a big surprise.'

'Then even if he's come to Peacebourne he won't be able to find me, will he?'

'Oh! We never thought of that.'

'We were in such a state.'

'And we remembered how he always has such faith in you, Mother. We reckoned you would be the one he'd turn to in a crisis.'

'Especially a love affair crisis.'

'Though of course we can't really be sure until we talk to him. But if he's done anything daft . . .!'

'Well, I haven't seen him. Sorry. But he's an intelligent lad and if he really wants to find me I've no doubt he will. Once he realises I've moved he'll probably turn up at the estate agent's, so I'll just pop back in there and tell them to send him over to the flat. Then I'll go there and wait for him while you drive out to the old house to see if he's there.'

Trust Mother to get everything organised with alacrity! Steve thought fondly.

Promising to meet up again soon, Harry's parents waved Kate off in her car, then walked across the street to where their own car was parked. Steve was just about to hand his wife into the front passenger seat when Harry rounded a corner at the other end of the street and spotted them.

Harry gave a great shriek of dismay.

'It's Dad and that awful woman! And the brazen cheek of it! She's wearing Mum's leather jacket!'

He grabbed his cousin's arm.

'Come on, let's scarper!'

'Wait a minute – let's at least see what she looks like!'

Amy started forward, eager to set eyes on this wicked marriage-breaker but Harry was wild to be gone. He took a firmer hold on Amy and began dragging her back.

'Hang about, Harry, I've just had a brainwave! I think I can guess what might have happened . . .' Amy began.

'I don't want to know. I don't want to have anything to do with her EVER!' Harry had no intention of coming face to face with his enemy until he had gleaned spiritual reinforcements from his gran.

Harry began hauling his cousin away,

aiming for the shelter of a nearby arcade, but Amy managed to wrench her hand free. She didn't like being pulled about so roughly, and anyway there was something really familiar about that woman. Keen to take a closer look, Amy darted off towards the car which still hadn't moved.

'Hey! Come back!' yelled Harry angrily. He guessed his cover had been blown and knew his dad must be looking for him. Once Steve spotted Amy he would guess the two of them were together. The game would be up; they would both be caught and driven back home before they'd even set eyes on Gran. Harry shuddered at the thought of actually having to live in the same house as that awful, thieving woman!

Yet Amy was determined to reach that car. For one thing, maybe Uncle Steve would know where Gran was. She had almost made it when the car suddenly started up and drove away.

8

Pride Before a Fall

As she unlocked the door of her new flat, Kate Bliss couldn't help a terrible sinking feeling. There was so much still to do and most of it couldn't be done until she mastered all the ultra-modern equipment with which she had been determined to start her new life.

'No half measures!' she had vowed. 'Now that I've decided to make a move I must catapult myself forward into the twenty-first century with a vengeance!'

Yet now she was beginning to wonder if she had moved a bit too fast for her own good. Her former home, in which she had lived for over forty years, had suffered from a severe lack of modernisation. So now everything was strange, from the bagless vacuum cleaner to the dimmer switches. She had moved from a single simple party-line telephone to a vastly complicated system with plugs in every room, handsets you could wander about with and easily mislay, and a message-recorder with a strange man's voice on it which kept saying she wasn't in when she certainly was.

Even basic things like the central heating seemed to have a will of their own, and as for all these smart-looking kitchen facilities, the dish-washer and the waste-disposal unit quite frankly terrified her and she seemed to spend all her time opening the wrong cupboard doors. Worse still, she had never used an electric cooker before, let alone a microwave, and yearned for her old smelly gas stove where pro-gress was reassuringly visible. She had never come close to setting the kitchen on fire with that, or ruined a meal on it as had been her experience here.

Kate Bliss had intended to take her time about coming to terms with all this, recruiting help with the major problems, but now, with Steve and his family about to turn up unexpectedly she was beginning to panic. The place was still in a chaotic mess, not at all the way she had wanted them to see it for the first time. She had so much yearned to impress her visitors, especially those worldly-wise grandchildren of hers who seemed to know everything about everything. She longed for them to admire the way she had kept up with the march of progress instead of regarding her as an ignorant, old-fashioned has-been.

Why, she had even bought a computer but it had scared her so badly that she had unplugged it completely and covered it over with a couple of old pillowcases lest the spirit within should escape from it while she was asleep. It certainly had a spirit, for that computer knew exactly what she was thinking. When she had tried to write a letter on it a message had appeared saying: 'You seem to be writing a letter . . .' Uncanny! Frightening! Weird!

Kate's great moment was supposed to arrive with the flat-warming party several weeks hence, by which time she had been hoping all would be well. Even that would have been a desperate struggle, but now she didn't even have that much time. Steve and Fran – and worse still, Harry – might be here in as little as half an hour. She must move fast, or be found out for the helpless, ignorant creature that she was.

Lifting the pillowcases gingerly from the sleeping computer, she decided to tidy them away in the airing cupboard until her guests had gone. Unfortunately, the sight of that naked, all-knowing screen put her into such a panic that she turned too quickly and caught her foot in the cord of the new bagless vacuum cleaner. This she had abandoned in the middle of the floor whilst trying to fathom out how to divest it of its accumulated fluff, there being no paper container to be tidily lifted out.

Down went Kate, falling heavily onto a boxful of crockery only half-unpacked.

9

Second Accident

Amy watched in dismay as Uncle Steve's car sped off. Those two must be on their way to see Gran, otherwise why come to Peacebourne? Still, Amy had failed to catch them, and being broke there was nothing she could do about it. No leaping into a taxi and yelling: 'Follow that car!'

She was just deciding to go back and look for Harry when there was a great screech of brakes behind her, followed by a scream, a thud and a whole cacophony of shouts and running feet.

Someone had been hit by a car!

Someone in a green anorak.

Harry!

From all directions a crowd closed in around a boy's body which lay face down and motionless in the road.

For a few seconds Amy stood paralysed with horror as the awful truth sank in. Then she sprang to life, yelling, 'Harry! HARRY!' as she tried to fight her way through the throng.

It was impossible. A police car had already turned up and the crowd was being urged to move back. Then almost immediately an ambulance came and whisked the boy away before Amy could make her presence felt.

At last, however, she managed to grab the attention of a policewoman who listened patiently while Amy explained that the victim was her cousin and that she wanted to be with him. The policewoman was about to leave for the hospital anyway to sort out the details of the accident, so she offered Amy a lift.

Amy hated hospitals. The very smell of them was enough to make her feel sick – which reminded her of her own predicament. But Harry could be in an even worse mess by now, so it was up to her to take a deep, brave breath. Filled with dread, she followed the policewoman across a packed hall and into a lift.

After traversing several blindingly white corridors they eventually arrived at a ward, the end bed of which had bright yellow curtains pulled around it.

'That's where he'll be!'

A few quick words with the sister in charge, then the policewoman marched down the ward, lifted a corner of the curtain and beckoned Amy forward. Amy immediately closed her eyes, trying to prepare herself for whatever horrors might lie in wait.

'Don't worry, dear, it's not that bad!' smiled the officer, putting an arm round Amy's shoulders and urging her forward.

'I've seen lots worse than this, I can tell you.'

Amy opened her eyes, took a deep, deep breath and slowly, courageously turned her head towards the figure in the bed.

It wasn't Harry!

10

The Clue of the Muddy Footprints

Steve's car bumped its way up the muddy lane to Kate's old house.

'Can't say I'm sorry she's moved at last,' Steve observed as the tyres began to struggle. 'I never could understand why Mum had to stay shut away up here once she was on her own. It was fine for us when we were kids, all that space to play in, but I certainly couldn't be doing with it now.'

'Oh, it's a lovely house. I've always liked it. Just look at the view, for a start!'

'I'd rather be looking at Harry. That boy has a lot of explaining to do. We've already wasted a whole day chasing after him. I'm supposed to be at a finance meeting.'

Muttering crossly, Steve climbed out, slammed the car door and began prowling round the house, peering in as the children had done before him.

'Well, he's certainly not here.'

'Someone's been snooping around very recently, though,' observed Fran, following behind with more care. 'Look at these footprints.'

'Could be anyone's. Builders, removal men, Gas Board.' Steve was in no mood to be pacified.

'Well, there are two lots of smallish, unworkmanlike prints, one with feminine heels. His and the problem girl-friend's, no doubt. If they're really desperate for help I guess they'll have gone off to the estate agent's now as your mother suggested. It's a wonder we didn't pass them on the way.'

'Right!' Steve responded grimly. 'In that

case they'll be at the flat by this time, so let's drop in on this touching twosome.'

Yet when they arrived at the flat there was no answer to their ring.

'Now what? Don't say Mum's disappeared as well!' Steve was growing more and more exasperated.

'She must be in; she promised to wait here in case Harry turned up. You don't think something's wrong, do you?'

'Plenty's wrong!'

'I mean with your mother.'

'What could be wrong with her? It's only half an hour since we left her, fit as a fireman.'

'Well, quite a lot can happen in half an hour.'

They rang several more times. At last they tried another doorbell and persuaded one of Kate's neighbours to let them into the hall. Given directions for flat No. 5, they hurried up the stairs. Fortunately Kate's main door was unlocked so they were able to walk in and find her lying unconscious on the floor, covered in splatters of blood and shards of broken crockery.

11

Relative Progress

At the foot of the curtained bed in the children's ward fat tears began to roll down Amy's cheeks. The policewoman thought these were tears of relief, since the boy in the bed was propped up looking bruised but fairly settled. After a quick glance at the chart hanging on the end of the bed, the officer put a consoling arm round Amy's shoulders.

'Cheer up, now; he's going to be fine, aren't you, Darren? Nothing serious. Should be home in a few days.'

Between hiccupy sobs Amy managed to

point out that a terrible mistake had been made. This Darren wasn't her cousin after all; she had never seen him in her life before. Which meant that her real cousin and her gran both seemed to have disappeared and she herself was lost in more ways than one.

'My gran's moved house and I don't know where she's gone to.'

'Well, that's not a problem. We'll track her down in no time. Anyway, what about your parents? You've never mentioned them.'

As this seemed to upset Amy even more, the policewoman summoned a nurse and asked her to look after the girl until she herself had finished questioning Darren. Then, she promised, a visit to the police station would soon sort things out, ending in a happy reunion.

The busy nurse led Amy briskly back through the ward and along more corridors until they reached a door marked RELATIVES' ROOM.

'You wait in here, dear, until the officer collects you.'

'But I'm not a relative. I'm nothing to do with this Darren.'

'Oh, that doesn't matter.'

The nurse opened the door and ushered Amy in.

'I'll see if we can rustle up a cup of tea.'

It was a comfortable room, with pretty curtains, deep armchairs, a couple of fragrant flower arrangements, a television set in a corner and a pile of magazines on a table. But Amy didn't notice any of these things. She simply sank into the nearest chair and gloomily contemplated her black future, what there was left of it. Already she was beginning to notice strange, alarming symptoms such as racing pulse, dry mouth and trembling limbs.

The nurse would have liked to stay and cheer this sad girl up but unfortunately there was no time to spare. There were patients with much more urgent problems; important life-and-death decisions to be made and never enough people to make them. Reluctantly the nurse hurried away, closing the door gently behind her.

Amy wedged her head in the wing of an armchair and didn't raise it again, even when the door re-opened some time later and another nurse led in a couple of grown-ups. Ashamed of her puffy cheeks and swollen red eyes, Amy kept her face hidden away from the newcomers.

'I'm sure this young lady won't mind if you join her,' smiled the nurse. Turning to the couple, she added: 'Make yourselves comfortable. The doctor will be with you soon to tell you how your mother is.'

The door had scarcely closed again behind the nurse when a voice cried:

'Why, it's Amy!'

Amy stiffened, then slowly turned, and was amazed to see Uncle Steve and Auntie Fran.

12

Blissful Ignorance

Steve, Fran and Amy gathered around Kate's hospital bed. Kate was propped up against a pile of pillows and seemed highly embarrassed about the whole affair.

'This is all a big fuss about nothing,' Kate insisted. 'A few stitches here and there, that's all, and an overnight stay just to be on the safe side, seeing I had a slight case of concussion. And I do mean slight.'

'You gave us a big fright, Mother, just the same!'

'Lying unconscious in all that blood.'

'What if your door had been locked?'

'Or if we hadn't been around, chasing our son?'

If you hadn't been chasing your son, thought Kate, I wouldn't have panicked and this might never have happened at all.

Aloud she said: 'Well, I'm fine now, as you can see. So never mind me; what about Harry?'

'Still missing.'

'But at least we've caught up with Amy. Apparently she was the last to see him, earlier today.'

'We came up on the train together,' Amy explained. 'We were both coming to see you, Gran, but then we got separated and I don't know where Harry is now.'

Shamefaced, she was forced to explain her silly mistake about the road accident and the green anorak which looked like Harry's.

'So I presume he's gone off on some wild, irresponsible spree with his girl-friend, then?' snapped Steve. 'Very loyal of you not to mention her.'

'You're not thinking of Gretna Green, I hope?' joked Fran. 'I think they'd be under age, even for that.'

Steve looked thunderous.

'It's no laughing matter. I guess Harry thought his gran would put him and this girl up for a while until he broke the news to us, and then when he realised about Mother moving house . . .'

'Just a minute! What girl-friend?' interrupted Amy.

'Paul said . . .'

'The teacher said . . .'

'The note said . . .'

'You said . . .'

'No; *you* said . . .'

It was all very confusing.

'Well, if he hasn't got girl-friend trouble, why on earth did he shoot off up here?'

Amy case a sidelong glance at Auntie Fran's face and hair. She really did look different – younger and more attractive – though surely anyone with half an eye could see she was still Auntie Fran?

'I – er – I think he thought you two were splitting up.'

'Splitting up?' Fran began to laugh incredulously. 'Where on earth did he get that daft idea?'

'I don't really know.' Amy hadn't the heart to explain.

'How could he possibly have thought such a thing? You know, that makes me feel very ignorant, not to mention guilty,' admitted Fran. 'Fancy not knowing what was going on in my own son's head! I should have ditched my stupid vanity and taken him into my confidence.'

She groaned dramatically.

'What a pair of idiots we've been! We must make it up to him.'

Steven wasn't sure if his wife was including Harry or himself in the 'pair of idiots' but felt resentful anyway.

'We've got to find him first,' he snapped. 'Anyone got any bright ideas?'

'You could try the station, Steve, in case he's decided to go back home,' suggested

Fran. 'I'll wait here with Amy in case he turns up.'

'No; I think the flat's the best idea,' argued Amy. 'He'll track it down sooner or later. Why don't you two go and wait there, and I'll stay with Gran? Don't split up; Harry needs to see you two together at close quarters.'

To tell the truth all Amy wanted was to have Gran to herself for a little while, so that she could sort out her own problem. Gran seemed quite capable of a serious conversation despite the various strips of sticking-plaster with which her face and arms were festooned.

'All right!' Glancing impatiently at his watch, Steve came to a decision. 'We'll cruise around in the car for a while to see if we can spot him, then we'll go and wait at the flat. But if he hasn't turned up in another hour or so we're coming straight back here. And if you still haven't heard anything by then we're going to the police.'

Amy sighed with relief. An hour should be long enough for her purposes. If only she knew how to begin!

She needn't have worried; Gran was ready for her. As soon as Steve and Fran had disappeared she turned to Amy and demanded:

'Now, young lady, what's your problem? You didn't come chasing up here just to hold Harry's hand.'

It certainly didn't take an hour. After less than fifteen minutes Amy's mood had changed completely and an enormous smile had spread itself across her newly-relaxed and brightened face.

'Oh, thanks, Gran! You're so wise! You know everything.'

Gran laughed. 'Well now, that's just where you're wrong. I've proved my ignorance in a big way lately. There are things you know far, far more about than I do. Microwaves and computers, for a start.' She went on to explain the difficulties she was facing in her new modern flat.

'Oh, but that's different.'

'No, it isn't. I can be just as baffled and confused as you. We're all ignorant about something in this life. Best not to be ashamed of your ignorance, though, or you'll never get round to asking advice. You know what they say, "A trouble shared is a trouble halved"?'

Amy grinned broadly.

'Agreed! So as soon as you're fit Harry and I will give you some computer lessons and some cookery demonstrations on the microwave, plus help with whatever else is bothering you. No problem; I'll fix something with Harry as soon as I see him.'

As if on cue, Steve and Fran appeared at this moment with a shamefaced-looking Harry between them.

'Spotted him staring longingly into a cake-shop window,' Fran explained. 'He was so hungry, so concentrated on food, that he actually didn't recognise me. Fancy that – his own mother!'

(Here Fran couldn't help a little grin of secret triumph.)

'You know, I don't think either of them has had anything to eat since breakfast.'

Amy suddenly realised how hungry she was. Ravenous! Starving! She had somehow developed an appetite like an all-in wrestler.

'We ran out of money,' she confessed.

'Off you all go and have a meal, then,' ordered Kate. 'You can come back and see me later.'

'We'd better ring Amy's folks first. They must be frantic.'

'No; it's all right. They think I'm at the zoo with Chloë and Lauren. As long as I'm back by tonight it will be OK, and I'd honestly rather you didn't tell them where I've been.'

'Like that, is it?' asked Steve with mock severity. 'Somewhat embarrassing, eh? Did you think *your* folks were splitting up as well?'

'A sort of – personal matter,' muttered Amy.

'Never mind, I've put her straight now,' Kate intervened hastily. 'There's no need to make a big fuss. What they don't know they won't grieve. There are times when ignorance is bliss.'

Even her own ignorance, she reflected happily, for now, because of it, she would see far more of her grandchildren as they coaxed her forth into the twenty-first century.